Who Wants an Old Teddy Bear?

A Random House PICTUREBACK®

Who Wants an Old Teddy Bear?

By Ginnie Hofmann

Published in the United States by Random House, Inc., New York, and simultaneously in Canada by Random House of Canada Limited, Toronto.
Library of Congress Cataloging in Publication Data: Hofmann, Ginnie. Who wants an old teddy bear? SUMMARY: Andy at first rejects the teddy bear he is given for a present, but through a strange turnabout learns to love it. [1. Toys—Fiction. 2. Dreams—Fiction.] I. Title. PZ7.H6795Wh [E] 80-10445
ISBN: 0-394-83924-2 (B.C.); 0-394-83925-0 (trade); 0-394-93925-5 (lib. bdg.)
Manufactured in the United States of America A B C D E F G H I J   1 2 3 4 5 6 7 8 9 0

RANDOM HOUSE  NEW YORK

One day the mailman brought a package for Andy.
It was a present from his grandmother.

Andy ran to his room and tore off the wrapping
paper. He had been hoping for a toy rocket ship.

But there was no rocket ship inside the box.
Instead there was a teddy bear.

"Ugh!" said Andy. "Who wants an old teddy bear?"
And he kicked it aside and went outdoors to play.

Andy stayed up late that night. When Mother said
it was past his bedtime, Andy brushed his teeth…

...and went to sleep. The teddy bear still lay on the floor beside his bed.

In the middle of the night, Andy began to dream.
He dreamt he had a magic umbrella that carried him

out the window and sailing up into the sky. Andy looked
back. "Oh, oh!" he cried. "Teddy bears!"

There were big teddy bears and small teddy bears.
There were teddy bears behind every cloud!

They chased Andy through the night sky—far
away from his home.

All of a sudden the sun was shining.
The bears gave Andy's umbrella a push.

Down, down, down he floated....
He landed in a teddy bear town.

The bears were very surprised to see a little boy in town.
"Where do you think he came from?" they wondered.

The little bears looked friendly enough, but a big
dog barked at Andy.

Andy ran away from the dog. But he did not get far.

Grandma Bear picked him up…wrapped him in a box…

and took him to the post office. What an awful dream!

That day the mailbear brought a package for Arthur.
It was a present from his Grandma.

"Oh, boy! I hope it's an electric train set," said Arthur
as he tore the wrapping paper off the box.

Arthur was very surprised when he found *Andy* in the box.
Andy was even more surprised....

"Who wants an old umbrella boy, anyway?" said Arthur, and he gave Andy a kick.

Andy began to cry. "I'm *not* an umbrella boy," he said. "My name is Andy, and I want to go *home*!"

Arthur was sorry. "Don't cry," he said. "I'll play
with you. Come on, Andy, let's be friends."

Andy and Arthur played together until
Father said it was past Arthur's bedtime and

Mother said it was time for Andy to go home.
Arthur carried Andy up the stairs.

He brushed his teeth and got ready for bed.
Then he gave Andy a great big bear hug.

As Arthur climbed into bed, Andy waved good-by.
The magic umbrella carried him out the window...

…and up, up, up into the sky. Soon Andy was floating down to his own house.

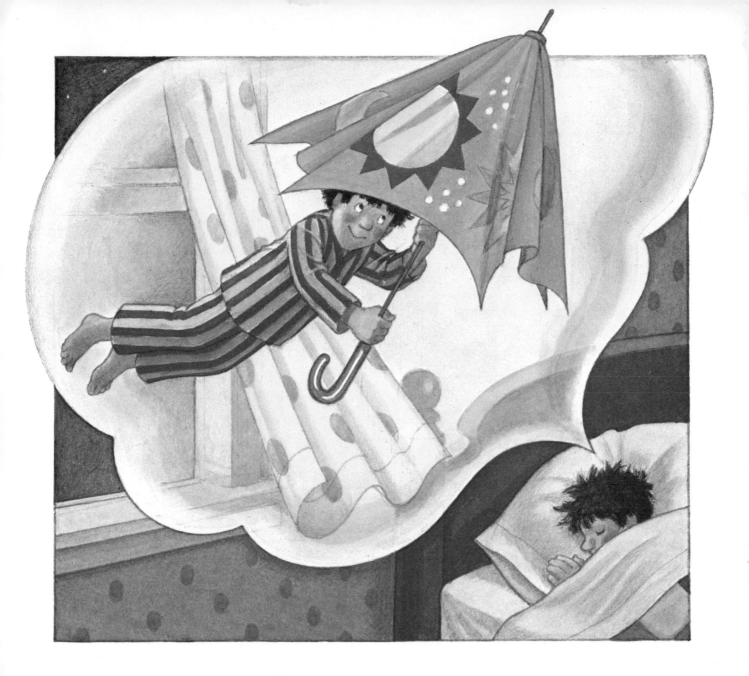

Andy floated through the window. His dream
was finally over, and it had ended happily.

Do you know who wants an old teddy bear, now?...
Andy does.